STARS OF SPORTS

LEWIS HAMILTON

RACING CHAMPION

■■▮ by Ryan G. Van Cleave

CAPSTONE PRESS
a capstone imprint

Published by Capstone Press, an imprint of Capstone
1710 Roe Crest Drive, North Mankato, Minnesota 56003
capstonepub.com

Library of Congress Cataloging-in-Publication Data is available on the Library of Congress website.
ISBN: 9781669076537 (hardcover)
ISBN: 9781669076759 (paperback)
ISBN: 9781669076766 (ebook PDF)

Summary: Learn about Lewis Hamilton's life, from childhood to professional racer.

Editorial Credits
Editor: Christianne Jones; Designer: Jaime Willems; Media Researcher: Svetlana Zhurkin; Production Specialist: Whitney Shaefer

Image Credits
Associated Press: Manu Fernandez, cover; Getty Images: Bryn Lennon, 24, Clive Mason, 5, 28, Dan Istitene, 15, Dan Mullan, 27, Formula 1/Dan Istitene, 18, Joe Portlock, 19, Lars Baron, 16, Mark Thompson, 7, Popperfoto/Philip Brown, 9, 10, SolStock, 26, Tommy Hilfiger/Jacopo Raule, 20; Newscom: Icon SMI/DPPI/Francois Flamond, 13, ZUMA Press/Sutton Motorsports, 11, 12; Shutterstock: cristiano barni, 17, Image Craft, 1, motorsports Photographer, 23, 25

Source Notes
Page 8, "He sacrificed . . ." Guest interview on HBO Real Sports with Bryant Gumbel, October 20, 2017, https://www.youtube.com/watch?v=GZVMTuSsEX4&ab_channel=HBO, Accessed July 3, 2023.

Page 8, "I was the only kid of color . . ." Maurice Peebles, "Lewis Hamilton: I Don't Need Your Validation," *Complex* magazine, September 23, 2016, https://www.complex.com/sports/a/maurice-peebles/lewis-hamilton-i-dont-need-your-validation, Accessed July 3, 2023.

Page 10, "I won the British Championship . . ." Charlotte Mathe, "10 Things About . . . Lewis Hamilton," digitalspy.com, July 12, 2014, https://www.digitalspy.com/showbiz/10-things-about/a582795/10-things-about-lewis-hamilton, Accessed July 3, 2023.

Page 21, "It's going to take all of us . . ." WE Staff. "Lewis Hamilton on climate change." we.org, https://www.we.org/en-GB/we-stories/we-day/this-earth-day-lewis-hamilton-is-fighting-climate-change, Accessed July 3, 2023.

Page 21, "Education doesn't just widen . . ." "Lewis Hamilton lines up with UNHCR in equality drive for refugee children's education," September 13, 2022, https://news.un.org/en/story/2022/09/1126521, Accessed July 3, 2023.

Page 24, "Silence is complicit . . ." Gary Younge, "Lewis Hamilton: 'Everything I'd suppressed came up—I had to speak out,'" *The Guardian.* July 10, 2021, https://www.theguardian.com/sport/2021/jul/10/lewis-hamilton-everything-id-suppressed-came-up-i-had-to-speak-out, Accessed July 3, 2023.

Page 27, "There are over 40,000 jobs across. . ." Gary Younge. "Lewis Hamilton: 'Everything I'd suppressed came up—I had to speak out,'" *The Guardian.* July 10, 2021, https://www.theguardian.com/sport/2021/jul/10/lewis-hamilton-everything-id-suppressed-came-up-i-had-to-speak-out, Accessed July 3, 2023.

Page 28, "He has nothing to prove . . ." Chris Heath, "Lewis Hamilton: The F1 Superstar on Racism, His Future, and the Shocker that Cost Him a Championship," *Vanity Fair*, August 8, 2022, https://www.vanityfair.com/style/2022/08/cover-story-lewis-hamilton-never-quits, Accessed July 3, 2023.

TABLE OF CONTENTS

Words in **BOLD** are in the glossary.

FAST LANE TO FAME

At the Brazilian Grand Prix in 2008, Lewis Hamilton found himself falling behind. He didn't need to win this race to secure his first Formula One (F1) World Championship. All he needed was a top-five finish. Yet in the final laps, he'd dropped to sixth. The tension ran high, and the crowd held its breath.

Then the skies opened up. Rain poured, making the track slick. Hamilton's car skidded and splashed, his tires struggling to grip the asphalt. Other drivers pulled into the **pit** to get fresh, dry tires. Hamilton didn't.

Hamilton chose correctly. In the final lap, he roared past the Toyota car. He snagged fifth place and won the championship—by just one point.

>>> Lewis Hamilton races ahead of driver Timo Glock in the 2008 Brazilian Grand Prix.

At 23 years old, Lewis Hamilton had become the youngest F1 World Champion ever. Hamilton was also the first Black F1 driver in history.

CHAPTER ONE

A SPEEDY START

Lewis Carl Davidson Hamilton was born on January 7, 1985, in Stevenage, England. His mother, Carmen, is white. His father, Anthony, is Black. Both of his parents are British. His parents separated when he was two years old. First, he lived with his mom. A few years later, he moved in with his dad. It wasn't easy.

When Hamilton was 6 years old, he received a remote-controlled car. He sent it zooming through the house. He raced his car against adults at the local track. He beat them. He even raced his car on a British children's TV show. His dad was shocked by his son's hand-eye coordination and racing ability.

FACT

Hamilton was named after the U.S. Olympic sprint champion Carl Lewis.

>>> Hamilton with his father
after a 2007 race.

On his seventh birthday, Hamilton got a **go-kart**. It wasn't new, but that didn't matter. He had no problem driving it. From that moment, his father decided to do everything he could to support his son's gift. Soon he was working four jobs to pay for Hamilton's racing dreams. And he served as a mechanic too. He would work on his son's go-karts until 3:00 a.m.

"He sacrificed every single penny, every second of his day," Hamilton said, "to give me the opportunity to shine."

As the only Black kid in the sport of racing, Hamilton faced **racism** and bullying. "I was the only kid of color on the track," he explained. "And I'd be getting pushed around. But then I could always turn their energy against them. I'd out-trick them, outsmart them, outwit them and beat them, and that, for me, was more powerful than any words."

And he kept on winning race after race after race.

〉〉〉 Hamilton races his go-kart in England in 1995.

Scary Spiders

Hamilton isn't scared of speed. He drives 200 miles (322 kilometers) per hour on the race track. He isn't scared of taking risks. He loves skydiving, rock climbing, and surfing. But he is terrified of spiders. He blames his sister, who made him watch the movie *Arachnophobia*.

CHAPTER TWO

A RISING STAR

Hamilton was a racing **prodigy**. He became the youngest driver to win the British Kart Championship in the cadet class at ten years old. That same year, he met Ron Dennis, the McLaren Formula One team owner. "I won the British Championship and one day I want to be racing your cars," Lewis told him. Dennis said to phone him in nine years.

〉〉〉 Ten-year-old Hamilton in his go-kart before a race

>>> Hamilton holding the McLaren Mercedes Champions of the Future trophy in 1996.

Hamilton's winning streak continued. In 1996, he won the McLaren Mercedes Champions of the Future series. He became Sky TV KartMasters Champion and Five Nations Champion too. The next year, he won even more awards. He became the British cadet karting champion again.

In 1998, Dennis signed Hamilton to the McLaren-Mercedes Young Driver Support Programme. Best of all, the offer included an option for a future Formula One seat.

Hamilton was ready for it. By age 15, he was the youngest driver to be ranked number one in karting. It was time to graduate from karts to cars.

In 2001, Hamilton had the chance to test a Formula Renault car for Manor Motorsport. After three laps, he crashed. Hamilton went right back to the track and kept working hard. He refused to quit.

〉〉〉 Hamilton drives a Renault car in England in 2001.

》》》 Hamilton at the 2006 GP2 championship.

FACT

Hamilton rarely drives outside the race track. He can't stand traffic!

Hamilton captured the 2003 British Formula Renault race series championship by winning 10 of the 15 races he entered. His success didn't stop there. In 2004, he progressed to the Formula Three Euroseries and won the championship the following year. In 2006, he won the Grand Prix 2 (GP2) championship.

No one doubted it now. Hamilton was a rising star in the racing world.

CHAPTER THREE

RACING TO THE TOP

The start of Hamilton's F1 career was astounding. In 2007, he was a **rookie** for the McLaren team. He was the first driver to finish on the podium in each of his first nine races. He was in the top spot. Then he had tire failure in China and a gearbox malfunction in Brazil. Those events ended up costing Hamilton the 2007 World Championship by a single point. This made him even more determined to win it all, and it didn't take him long.

He won five races in 2008. He won his first World Championship with a bold move on the last corner of the final lap of the deciding race.

In 2013, Hamilton shocked everyone by switching to the Mercedes-AMG Petronas team. He **dominated** the sport, winning World Championships in 2014, 2015, 2017, 2018, 2019, and 2020. This tied him with Michael Schumacher for the most ever. Hamilton has since passed Schumacher for the most Grand Prix wins.

〉〉〉 Hamilton recognizing the crowd after winning the F1 Abu Dhabi Grand Prix in 2019.

〉〉〉 Hamilton congratulates Verstappen on his World Championship win in 2021.

Hamilton nearly won an eighth World Championship in 2021. However, a judge's **controversial** decision got in the way. The call allowed Dutch driver Max Verstappen to make a pit stop and get fresh tires for the last lap. He overtook Hamilton on the final lap and won the race. Despite the unfairness, Hamilton acted like a true champion. He personally congratulated the 24-year-old Dutch driver.

Whether he wins an eighth World Championship or not, Hamilton is already one of the most successful F1 race car drivers of all time.

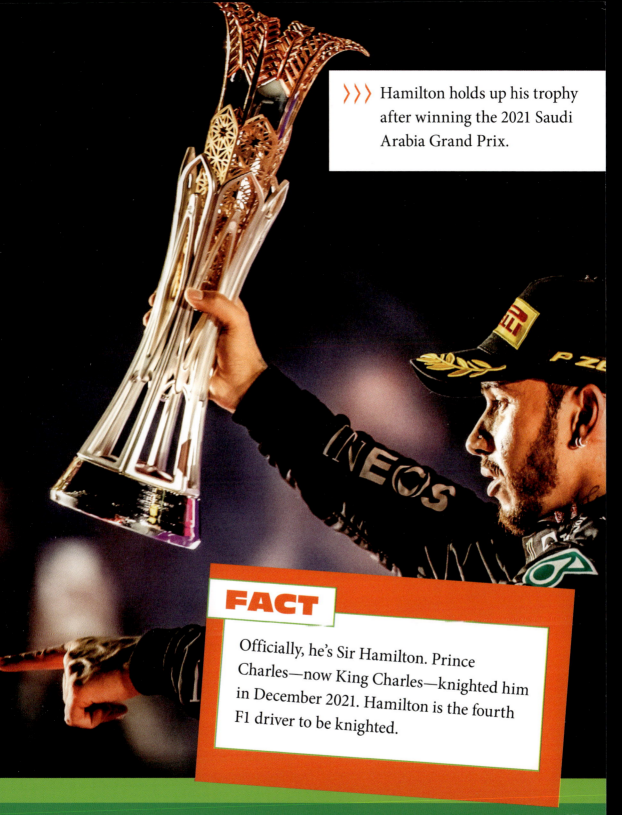

》》》 Hamilton holds up his trophy after winning the 2021 Saudi Arabia Grand Prix.

FACT

Officially, he's Sir Hamilton. Prince Charles—now King Charles—knighted him in December 2021. Hamilton is the fourth F1 driver to be knighted.

CHAPTER FOUR

MAKING A DIFFERENCE

Despite his fame, Hamilton is a low-key, down-to-earth person. He spends a lot of time on community and charity work. He supports organizations like UNICEF and the World Wildlife Fund.

>>> Hamilton (front row, fourth from the left) and other F1 drivers pose with a banner supporting UNICEF in 2022.

Hamilton is a big advocate for animal welfare and veganism. He's the only **vegan** F1 driver. He spreads the word about the benefits of a vegan lifestyle. He's also working to have Mercedes stop using animal-sourced leather in its cars.

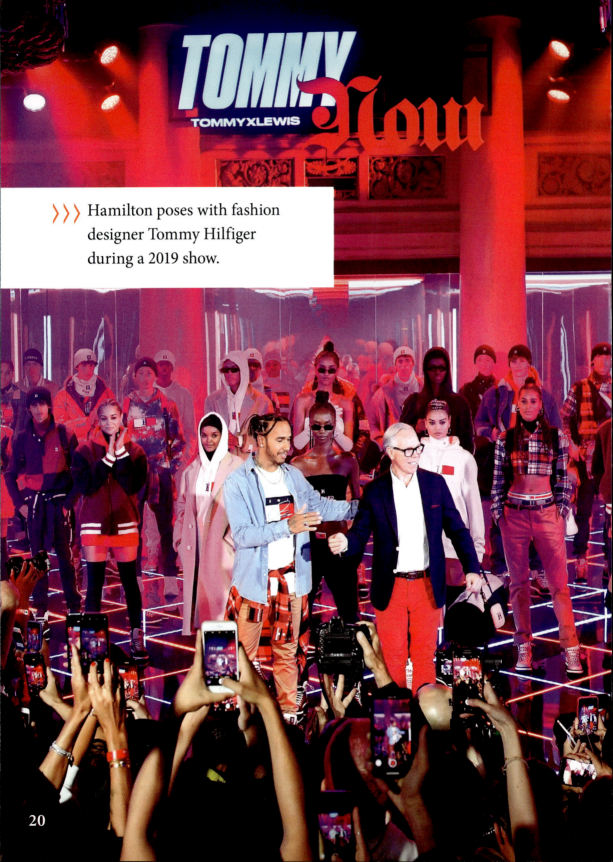

》》》 Hamilton poses with fashion designer Tommy Hilfiger during a 2019 show.

Hamilton is also passionate about the environment. He uses his clothing collections with designer Tommy Hilfiger to promote **sustainable** practices. He urges young people to fight global climate change.

"It's going to take all of us to come together, being united, to make small changes in our lives," he says. "We're so fortunate to have and occupy this planet, so we better start treating it right."

Most recently, Hamilton is lending his support to the United Nations' campaign for refugee children and youth in schools. "Education doesn't just widen people's horizons and present them with opportunities they would otherwise never dream of getting," he said. "It counteracts the damaging effects of **systemic injustice**."

FACT

Hamilton donated $500,000 to support firefighters and animal welfare organizations during the 2020 Australian bushfires.

CHAPTER FIVE

POWERFUL BEYOND MEASURE

Hamilton continues to make a name for himself beyond the track. He sits in the front row at fashion shows. He's photographed with celebrities. He secretly records hundreds of songs he's written or cowritten.

He isn't afraid to speak out for change. In his autobiography, Hamilton wrote, "For me, race is not an issue at all." But that was what he was encouraged to say.

Thesc days, he no longer lets others tell him what to do, say, or wear. He is fully committed to speaking out against racism no matter what F1 or sponsors prefer.

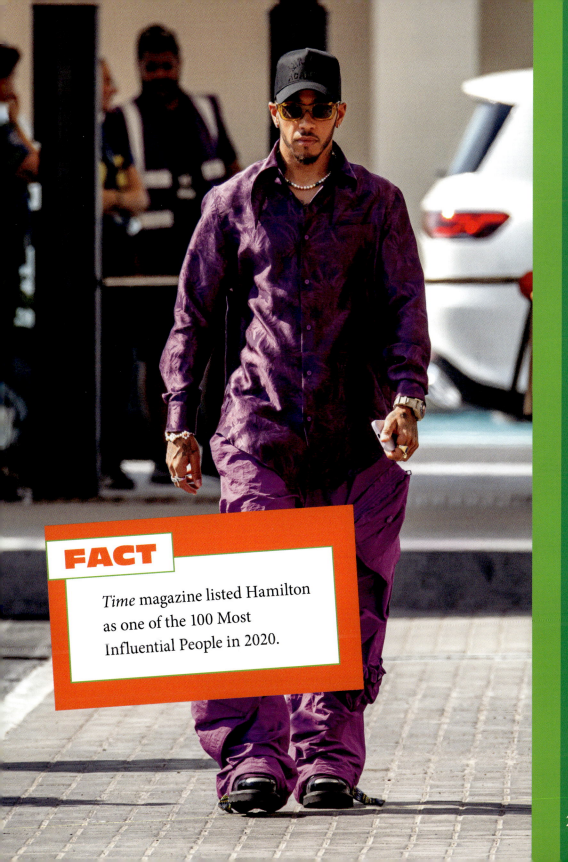

FACT

Time magazine listed Hamilton as one of the 100 Most Influential People in 2020.

>>> Hamilton (center) and other F1 drivers show their support for the Black Lives Matter movement in 2020.

After the tragic death of George Floyd in 2020, Hamilton made international headlines. He wore a "Black Lives Matter" T-shirt. He convinced 12 other drivers to wear "End Racism" shirts. "Silence is **complicit**," he told them. He continued to stand against racism by raising his fist in the Black Power salute after winning the Styrian Grand Prix.

A tattoo across his chest reads "Powerful Beyond Measure." It reminds Hamilton that he needs to do meaningful things with his money, fame, and power.

Meaningful Tattoos

Hamilton's chest tattoo comes from this quote by writer Marianne Williamson: "Our deepest fear is not that we are inadequate. Our deepest fear is that we are powerful beyond measure. It is our light, not our darkness, that most frightens us." He also has the phrase "Still I Rise" tattooed on his upper back and written on his helmet. That is the title of a poem by poet and activist Maya Angelou.

>>> Chemistry is an important part of STEM-related classes.

Hamilton did more than protest. In 2021, he launched Mission 44. He donated $25 million to start the foundation. This charitable organization seeks to empower young people from underserved groups to succeed. He also created a partnership between Mission 44 and the Mercedes team. It is called Ignite. It seeks to increase diversity in STEM fields that could lead to careers in motorsports.

Hamilton said, "There are over 40,000 jobs across motor sports in the UK, and less than 1% are filled by people from Black backgrounds. So there's a lot of opportunity in so many different categories, not just engineering."

>>> The Mercedes team supports its drivers on and off the track.

FACT

In 2020, Hamilton won the Laureus World Sportsman of the Year Award. The following year, he became the first winner of the Laureus World Sports Awards Athlete Advocate of the Year Award for his fight against racism.

In February 2024, Hamilton surprised the world by signing with Ferrari for the 2025 season. After that, who knows what will happen? Hamilton's close friend and Olympic fencer Miles Chamley-Watson has an idea: "He has nothing to prove but a lot more to accomplish. And I think he's just going to keep going until the wheels fall off, literally."

〉〉〉 Hamilton interacts with fans during the drivers' parade before the 2023 Japanese Grand Prix.

TIMELINE

1985   Born in Stevenage, England, on January 7

1991   Receives first remote-controlled car, sparking interest in racing

1993   Begins racing go-karts

1998   Joins McLaren-Mercedes Young Driver Support Programme, becoming the youngest driver to secure a professional contract

2001   Debuts in British Formula Renault Winter Series

2003   Wins the British Formula Renault Winter Series

2005   Wins the European Formula 3 Championship

2006   Wins the GP2 Series Championship

2007   Makes Formula One debut with McLaren

2008   Becomes youngest F1 World Champion

2013   Joins the Mercedes-AMG Petronas F1 Team

2014   Wins second World Championship (first with Mercedes)

2015   Wins third World Championship

2020   Wins seventh World Championship, tying the record with Michael Schumacher

2021   Becomes first winner of the Laureus World Sports Awards Athlete Advocate of the Year Award

2024   Signs with Ferrari for the 2025 season

GLOSSARY

COMPLICIT (kuhm-PLIH-suht)—to help or allow something wrong to happen

CONTROVERSIAL (kahn-truh-VER-shuhl)—describing something that causes disagreements or arguments

DOMINATE (DOM-uh-neyt)—to rule

GO-KART (GOH-kart)—a small, open-wheel vehicle used for racing

PIT (PIT)—a place alongside a racecourse where drivers stop to refuel or fix their cars

PRODIGY (PROD-i-jee)—a young person who has extraordinary talent or ability

RACISM (REY-siz-uhm)—thinking that a particular racial group is better than another

ROOKIE (ROOK-ee)—a first-year player

SUSTAINABLE (suh-STEY-nuh-buhl)—a method of using a resource so it is not permanently damaged or destroyed

SYSTEMIC INJUSTICE (sih-STEH-mik in-JUH-stuhs)—unfairness or wrong doing built into the way a society works

VEGAN (VEE-guhn)—someone who chooses not to eat or use any products from animals, including meat, dairy, eggs, and sometimes clothes made from animal products

READ MORE

Cain, Harold P. *Lewis Hamilton: Auto Racing Star*. Lake Elmo, MN: Focus Readers, 2023.

Jones, Bruce. *Formula One 2022: The World's Bestselling Grand Prix Guide*. London: Welbeck Publishing, 2024.

Mikoley, Kate. *Lewis Hamilton*. New York: Gareth Stevens Publishing, 2023.

INTERNET SITES

Formula One: Lewis Hamilton
formula1.com/en/drivers/lewis-hamilton.html

The Hamilton Commission
hamiltoncommission.org

Mercedes-AMG Petronas Formula One Team
mercedesamgf1.com

INDEX

AUTHOR BIO

Ryan G. Van Cleave is the author of dozens of books for children and hundreds of articles published in magazines. As The Picture Book Whisperer, they help celebrities write books for children. Ryan lives in Florida.